to Yoko

with special thanks to
Janice Thomson

First published in Great Britain by Andersen Press Ltd., 2007
Printed and bound in Singapore
First American edition, 2008
10 9 8 7 6 5 4 3 2 1

www.fsgkidsbooks.com

Library of Congress Cataloging-in-Publication Data
Lucas, David, date.
    The robot and the bluebird / David Lucas.— 1st American ed.
        p. cm.
    Summary: A broken robot makes a home for a cold, tired bluebird trying to
fly south for the winter, and eventually he carries the bird to a warmer climate while
she rests in the cavity where his heart used to be.
    ISBN-13: 978-0-374-36330-7
    ISBN-10: 0-374-36330-7
    [1. Robots—Fiction. 2. Birds—Fiction.] I. Title.

PZ7.L96895Ro 2008
[E]—dc22

2007026930

DAVID LUCAS

The Robot and the Bluebird

FARRAR STRAUS GIROUX
NEW YORK

There once was a Robot
with a *broken* heart.

The others did their best to fix him,
but it wasn't any good.

So he was sent to sit on the scrap heap
with all the other old machines.

He tried talking to them.
He said, "My heart was broken, you know."
But they didn't answer.

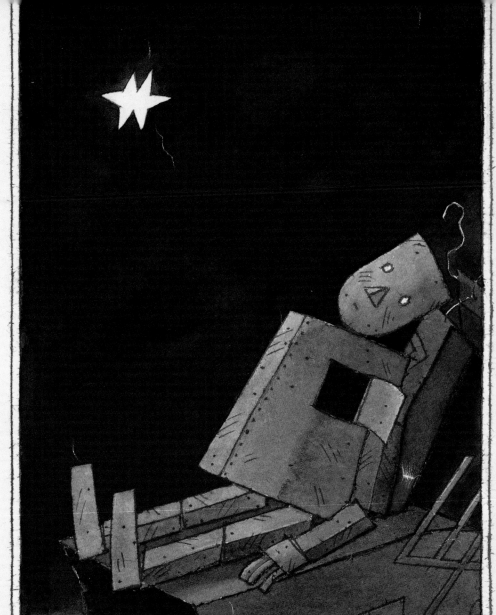

So he lay down and looked up at the sky.
He lay there through the long, dark nights and the empty days.

He lay there rusting in the autumn rain.
He lay there when the first snows of winter fell.

And there, one day, was a Bluebird, fighting against the freezing wind.
She landed on his shoulder.

"What are you doing here, little bird?" he said.
"I'm flying south," she said weakly. "South, where the sun shines.
But I'm so cold and tired I can go no farther."
"I'm sure you don't want to stay here," said the Robot. "I'm rubbish."
But the Bluebird just shivered and said nothing.

"There's a space where my heart used to be,"
the Robot said gently. "You can sleep there if you like."

So the Bluebird settled down to sleep
on a nest the Robot made.

And as the Robot looked out into the night,
he was astonished to feel as if he had a warm, living, beating heart.
And when the Bluebird fluttered,
he felt as if his own heart were fluttering.

The next morning, the door to his heart opened
and the Bluebird sang, sweet and bright in the icy air.

"My old heart only ever said *ticktock*," said the Robot,
"but now my heart is *singing*."

And the Bluebird flew a little way up into the air,
and the Robot felt like his heart was *flying*.
And, creaking, he got to his feet,
and danced a creaking, clanking dance.

"I wish I could live in your heart,"
said the Bluebird,
"but I'll die of cold if I stay here.
Winter has come so soon
and I still have so far to go.
I don't even know if I have the strength,"
she said sadly,
settling in his hand.

"Then let me carry you," said the Robot.
"I'll carry you in my heart,
    and shelter you from the cold and storms."

And so he carried her in his heart,
across frozen wastes,
over towering mountains,
through blizzards and fog,
until he was deathly tired
and his joints groaned with every step.

And when at last the sun shone,
he opened the door to his heart
and out flew the Bluebird,
singing and twittering thank-yous.

The Robot lifted his arms toward her,
but he couldn't take another step.
His strength had failed at last.
"Make your home in my heart,"
he said in the faintest whisper,
and he hung his head.

And the Bluebird lived in his heart *always*.

And the Robot stands there still,
his arms outstretched
like an old, hollow tree,
home every year
to singing birds.